I Love My Papi!

by Alison Inches
illustrated by Dave Aikins

Ready-to-Read

Simon Spotlight/Nick Jr.

New York   London   Toronto   Sydney

Based on the TV series *Dora the Explorer*® as seen on Nick Jr.®

SIMON SPOTLIGHT
An imprint of Simon & Schuster Children's Publishing Division
1230 Avenue of the Americas
New York, New York 10020
Copyright © 2004 Viacom International Inc.
Manufactured in the United States of America
First Edition
2 4 6 8 10 9 7 5 3 1
Library of Congress Cataloging-in-Publication Data
Inches, Alison.
I love my Papi! / by Alison Inches ; illustrated by Zina Saunders.—1st ed.
p. cm. — (Ready-to-read)
"Based on the TV series Dora the Explorer as seen on Nick Jr."
Summary: Dora and her Papi play baseball, go to the beach, read books, and do lots of
other fun things together.
ISBN 0-689-86495-7
[1. Fathers and daughters—Fiction.] I. Saunders, Zina, ill. II. Dora the explorer
(Television program) III. Title. IV. Series.
PZ7.I355 Iae 2004
[E]—dc22
2003014360

My  PAPI and I love to do things together!

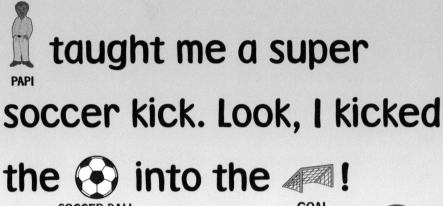 taught me a super soccer kick. Look, I kicked the  into the !

PAPI

SOCCER BALL

GOAL

We also love playing  .
BASEBALL

PAPI coaches my team.

He taught us how to
swing the  and slide

BAT

into home
.

BASE

On weekends  and I ride **BIKES** together.

PAPI

Or sail on a  .
BOAT

Sometimes we go to the  together.

BEACH

We build giant and
SAND CASTLES

play in the .
WAVES

My 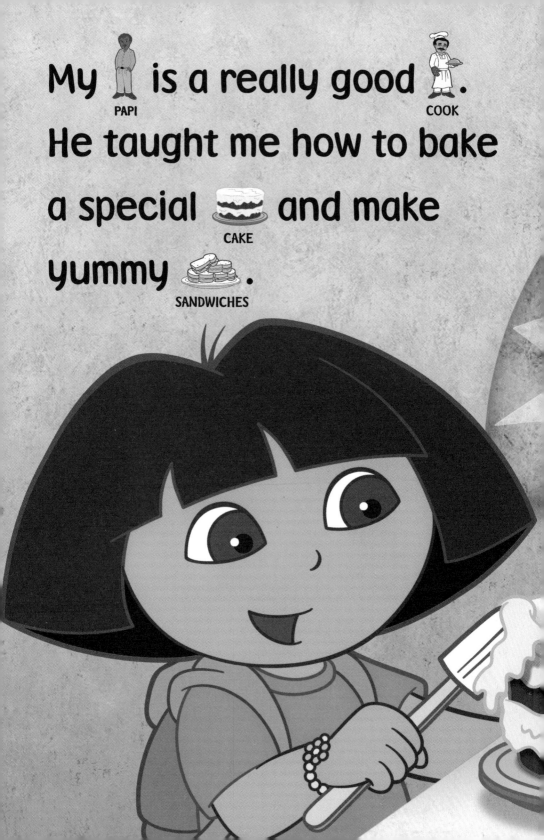 **PAPI** is a really good **COOK**.
He taught me how to bake
a special **CAKE** and make
yummy **SANDWICHES**.

Sometimes we pack a  PICNIC

and share it with my

friend BOOTS .

My  **PAPI** made us this **TIRE** swing! He can build anything with **TOOLS**.

One time  took us to
the 🎪 . 🐒 loved the 🤡🤡 .

PAPI

CIRCUS   BOOTS   CLOWNS

Then bought us and

PAPI

POPCORN

  for a treat.

STRAWBERRY ICE CREAM

Yum! Yum!

At the end of every day   tucks me into 🛏.

PAPI

BED

Then we read a .
BOOK
I like BOOKS about ANIMALS.

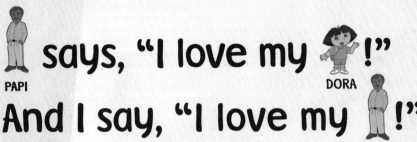 says, "I love my !"

And I say, "I love my !"